Scholastic Children's Books
Euston House, 24 Eversholt Street
London NW1 1DB
A division of Scholastic Ltd
London ~ New York ~ Toronto ~ Sydney ~ Auckland
Mexico City ~ New Delhi ~ Hong Kong

First published in the USA by Scholastic Inc,. 2006
First published in the UK by Scholastic Ltd, 2006

Over the Hedge TM & © 2006 DreamWorks
Animation L.L.C

10 digit ISBN: 0 439 95120 8
13 digit ISBN: 978 0 439 95120 3

All rights reserved
Printed by Nørhaven Paperback A/S, Denmark
2 4 6 8 10 9 7 5 3 1

MOVIE STORYBOOK

WRITTEN BY SARAH DURKEE
ILLUSTRATIONS BY PETE EMSLIE AND KOELSCH STUDIOS

SCHOLASTIC

RJ the raccoon needed food, and he needed it FAST. So he decided to steal some - even though the pile of food belonged to a sleeping, vicious, seven-foot bear.

It would have been a clean getaway, but RJ couldn't resist sampling one tiny snack from his haul.

Vincent the bear opened one yellow eye. He was furious. He couldn't believe

RJ had been dumb enough to try stealing his stuff. Then things got worse: Vincent's precious red trolley of food rolled down a hill and was flattened by a van!

"When the moon is full in one week," Vincent threatened, "I'm waking up again. And ALL my stuff had better be right back where it was, or I will hunt you down and kill you."

The next morning, the whole woodland family woke up to the first beautiful day of spring. Stella the skunk cleared everyone out of the log by doing what skunks do best. Ozzie the possum did what possums do best: played dead. His daughter Heather did what teenagers do best: died of embarrassment.

Verne, a sensible turtle with a good head on his shell, handed out the last of the food.

Then, he did what he did every year: He reminded everyone of the importance of finding food.

"Only 274 days left till winter!" he warned. Quillo, Spike, and Bucky – the porcupine kids – were raring to go. Hammy the squirrel ran off in search of the nuts he'd buried last autumn, and ran smack into something he'd never seen before. He tried to tell his friends right away.

When Hammy showed the rest of the animals the strange thing, they were scared . . . very scared.

It was tall and green. And it stretched in both directions, as far as they could see.

"I wouldn't be so scared if I just knew what it was called," said Penny, the porcupines' mum.

Verne took action. He worked up his courage, tripped, and fell right through the great and powerful Steve to the other side.

LET'S CALL IT STEVE!

AAAGGHHH

The other side of the hedge was a strange new world. A hundred brand-new houses stood where the woods had been. And that was just the beginning! A twisting garden hose flung Verne over a fence, and plopped him into the driver's seat of a toy car. He careered down the street and straight into the path of . . . a big, real car. Driven by a big, real, actual human.

"AAAAAH!" Verne howled as he shot under the huge car.

BAM! He slammed into a postbox, landing in the street next to a hockey puck.

FWAP! A rollerskating human slap-shot Verne straight through the air and back over the hedge.

Verne lay gasping on the ground as the animals ran over to help him.
"What was over there?" cried Ozzie.

"I think it was humans," Verne panted. But that wasn't the worst part, he said. Half the forest was gone. The animals listened in disbelief. How would they gather enough food for the winter?

"It's called a hedge," RJ suddenly said, "and it's the gateway to the good life!"
RJ told them they could fill their log – in a week!
"You just need a guide," RJ said. "We'll go over there tonight!"
The animals devoured RJ's tortilla chips, floating in a flavour cloud of bliss.
But Verne's tail tingled. That only happened when something was very wrong.

"Welcome to suburbia!" RJ crowed. The animals loved every perfect blade of grass. Then, they witnessed the astonishing ability of humans to consume food.

Everywhere the animals looked, there were overfed humans, grilling and chilling, dining and reclining, chomping, chewing, slurping, burping . . . EATING. And the stuff they *didn't* eat?

"They put it in gleaming, silver cans, just for us!" RJ said triumphantly. "Dig in!"

The animals dove into a rubbish bin feeding frenzy.
   Suddenly, they heard an electronic beep and froze. A huge cat stepped through an automatic cat flap, took one snotty look at the intruders, and let out a bloodcurdling "MEEEEEEOOOWWWW!"
   Then a woman, Gladys, burst out, waving a broom.

"Get outa here!" she screamed, swinging wildly.

The animals ran back through the hedge, breathless and terrified.

"We want nothing to do with ANYTHING that's over that hedge," Verne insisted.

Verne led his family away from RJ.

But RJ didn't give up easily. The next day, he came up with a plan, and it involved Hammy.

Shelby and MacKenzie were delivering Trail Guide Gals cookies using a trolley . . . a trolley exactly like the one RJ needed for Vincent.

"You're gonna be a vicious, man-eating, rabid squirrel," RJ instructed.

Hammy jumped up and down like a maniac and ran around in circles. "I WANT MY COOKIES!" he screeched at the girls.

Shelby and MacKenzie were no fools. They looked up "rabid squirrel" in their manual. Then they bashed Hammy over the head with it. Verne came to the rescue, but RJ came off looking like a hero.

RJ, Hammy, and a confused Verne rolled off with the trolleyload of cookies.

What a difference a sugar-rush makes. After the cookies, the animals pulled off heist after heist. Working together, they stole hot dogs, birthday cakes, bags of groceries . . . even electronic games, music players, and phones! Nobody but Verne wanted to forage in the woods anymore. He watched his family celebrate, as he sadly added his berries to the pile.

The screeching of tyres made Verne race to the road. Ozzie was lying "dead" on the pavement! But it was just a trick so the animals could steal a blue cool box that RJ needed for Vincent. The humans had had enough. Gladys came out of her perfect house and announced that she had called an exterminator. Not just any exterminator, but Dwayne LaFontaine.

Verne watched as RJ and the other animals carried the cool box back through the hedge. But with Dwayne on the case, Verne knew they would never be safe.

Back in the meadow, the animals congratulated Ozzie on his incredible performance.

"And let's not forget RJ," Ozzie reminded the crowd.

They led RJ to a fabulous room, complete with a TV and a special chair, just for him. Hammy popped open a can of pop and handed it to RJ. Heather even gave him the remote.

RJ had never been treated so well in his life. He felt like part of the family. He felt like they trusted him. He felt . . . awful. He went up the tree, to think.

"You should be ashamed of yourself!"

". . . say it aloud. I'm a dirtbag."

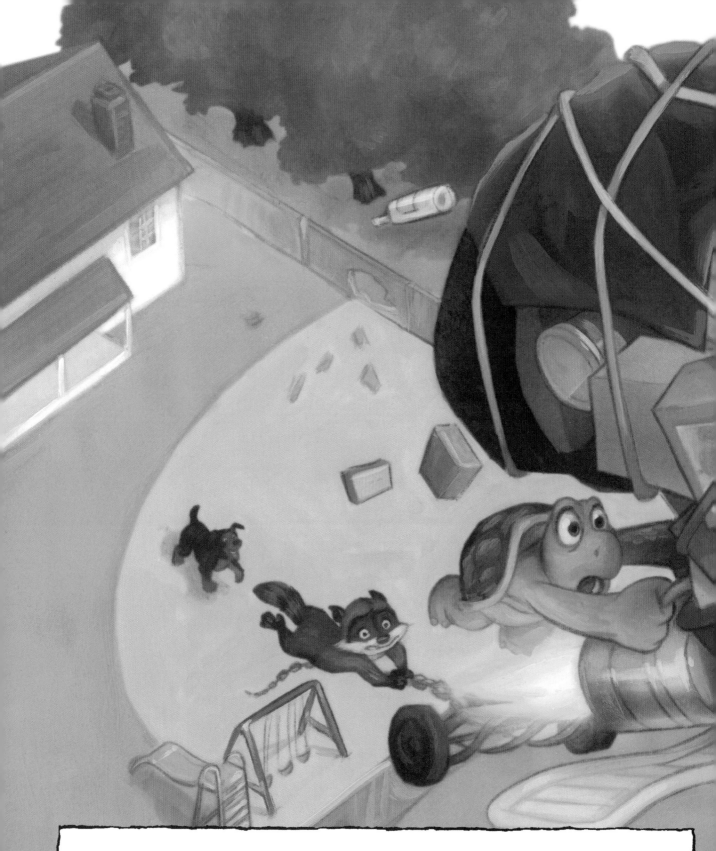

RJ couldn't believe his eyes. Verne had loaded the trolley with every single scrap of food and was determined to return it all to the humans.

"I'm giving this back so they won't kill us!" Verne said grimly.

RJ and Verne had a tug-of-war with the trolley.

"You don't understand!" RJ cried. "We NEED this stuff!"

Nugent the dog ended the argument.

"Play! Play! Play!" he insisted. He dragged them and the trolley all over the neighbourhood, until a gas canister exploded and sent the trolley rocketing skyward. It crash-landed, smashing everything to smithereens. Even RJ's precious crisps.

The animals blamed Verne for losing the food, and sided with RJ.

Verne, feeling hurt, did an extremely common hurt-feelings thing: he said something mean.

"You're taking advantage of them," he yelled at RJ, "because they're too stupid and naïve to know any better!"

The animals were stunned, especially Hammy.

They all walked away from Verne. Now it was Verne's turn to do some thinking.

Verne finally admitted it. He was jealous of RJ. They had a long talk.
"I have to make it up to them. I need to get the food back," Verne told RJ.
On the same team at last, RJ started to hatch a plan and Verne agreed to help. A plan to get all that food back in one night.

VRRRR

Meanwhile, Dwayne was all over the neighbourhood.

He'd put Gladys's garden into lockdown and installed the best thing in his arsenal: the Depelter Turbo – even though it was illegal in 48 states.

RRRRR

He armed the lasers and gutted a stuffed bunny to demonstrate.
Gladys smiled approvingly as the machine ripped the pelt right off.
They were ready.

In the meadow, the animals planned their biggest heist yet. They had to avoid all the traps. And they had to get inside Gladys's house. They just needed to get the collar from Tiger the cat! It opened the cat flap like an electronic key, RJ explained.

"And you, Stella, will get that cat to give you his collar by using . . ."
"My stink," said Stella.
"Your feminine charms!" RJ corrected.
It was extreme-makeover time for Stella.

Tiger found Stella so charming that getting the collar was a piece of cake. She flirted with Tiger to distract him while the animals snuck through the cat flap and into Gladys's house.

The animals moved fast. The porcupine kids set up a security camera to keep an eye on the sleeping Gladys.

"Penny, Lou, clean out that fridge! Ozzie, Heather, cabinets and pantry!" RJ ordered. The trolley filled up fast.

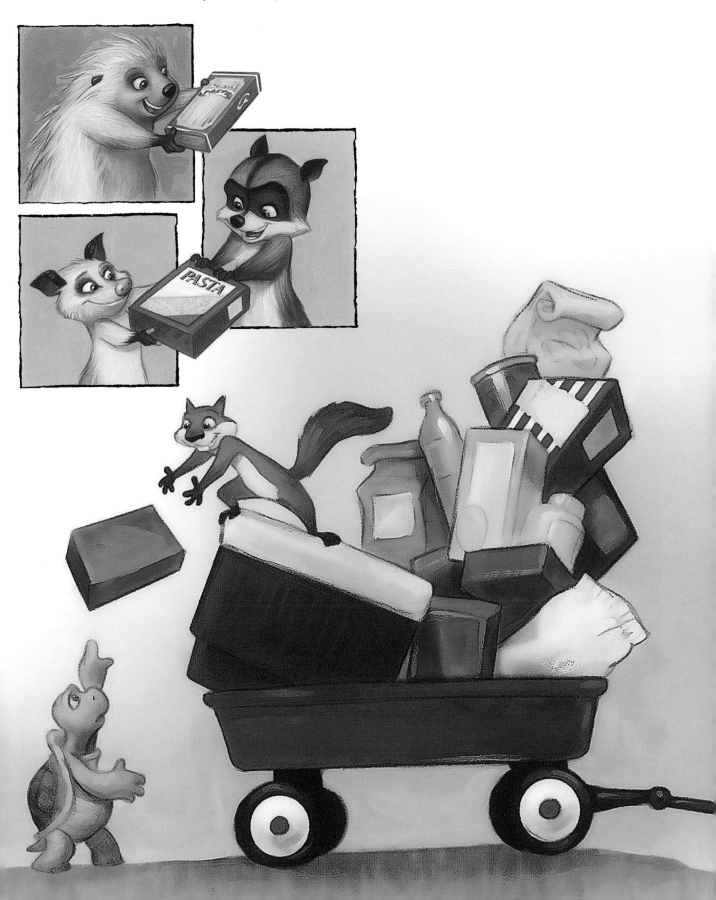

At the sound of the coffeemaker, Gladys shuffled into the kitchen, yawning. *Busted!* the animals thought. But she didn't even see them.

The trolley was loaded up and they were ready to scram. Then RJ saw a can of crisps, and there was no way he was going to leave without it.

"We have enough food!" Verne insisted.
"Hey listen, I've gotta deliver these crisps to a homicidal bear!" RJ snapped.
Now Verne knew what RJ was really up to. But there was no time to fight.
Gladys had seen them, and she called Dwayne LaFontaine.
"GET OVER HERE AND VERMINATE!" she screamed.

"I was on my way to kill you," growled Vincent, "but I stopped to watch the show."

RJ looked down the hill and, to his horror, saw that his friends were in trouble.

RJ knew what he had to do.

    RJ grabbed the trolley, leaped onto it, and tore off down the hill, straight
for Dwayne's van.
    CRASH! RJ landed on the bonnet of the van. Dwayne was knocked unconscious
    Vincent came barreling after RJ, hit the van, and knocked Verne into the
driver's seat.

"How do I control this thing?" Verne hollered, turning the wheel wildly. The porcupine kids took over.

"We'll drive," said Spike.

"It's just like our video game!" Quillo shouted happily.

They jumped on the wheel, sending the van spinning around.

"AAAAH!" the animals screamed as the van swerved, nearly throwing the battling Vincent and RJ off the roof. Vincent came after RJ with the giant hammer from the van's roof.

"Let me in!" begged RJ through the window.

"No, you ring-tailed charlatan!" shouted Ozzie.

"He's trying to help! My tail's not tingling anymore!" yelled Verne. The van crashed into a bunch of balloons at the entrance to El Rancho Camelot Estates, and Vincent got caught on them. He floated up, up, and away. The van hit a sign. The sign bent, creating a ramp.

Gladys came out of her house in time to see the van flying off the broken sign and into the air.

"AHHHH!" screamed RJ, Verne, and the now wide-awake Dwayne.

"AHHHH!" screamed Gladys.

The van crashed down into Gladys's house like a meteorite.

KA
BO

Dwayne and Gladys chased the animals into the hedge.

"Take care of your family, Verne," RJ gasped. But Verne was starting to think of RJ as family, too.

With the help of some pop, Hammy sprang into action. He was a total blur as he raced across the garden. He pushed the trap's

ON button, then bolted back to the hedge.

The animals donned safety gear to watch as the Depelter Turbo roared into life and exploded.

RJ popped some popcorn and shared it with Verne while the porcupine kids roasted marshmallows. Everyone enjoyed the show.

The exploding Depelter left a huge crater in the garden and locked Vincent, Gladys, and Dwayne in a steel cage.

Animal Control took Vincent away.

The police came and arrested Gladys for owning the highly illegal Depelter.

As for Dwayne . . . Nugent took care of him.

"Play?" said Nugent from the other side of the fence where Dwayne had gone to hide.

Justice is a beautiful thing.

Safe in the meadow, the animals were celebrating. RJ stood to one side, watching.

"Hey, RJ," Verne said. "Y'know, if you had only told us that you owed food to a bear, we would've just given it to you!"

RJ was shocked. Stunned. Blown away.

"This whole family thing is very confusing if you've never done it before," he said sheepishly.

"Family. *That's* the gateway to the good life." Verne smiled. "Wanna be part of it?"

RJ definitely did.

It was time for a group hug. Yes, even with quills.